THE
LATE CUCKOO

THE
LATE CUCKOO

BY

LOUIS SLOBODKIN

THE VANGUARD PRESS INC.

NEW YORK   NEW YORK

In a little Swiss village high up in the Swiss Alps there was once a little clockmaker's shop full of cuckoo clocks.

At every hour through the day and night, the cuckoo clocks would mark the hours as they passed.

At one o'clock they would strike one. At two o'clock they would strike two, and so on at each and every hour.

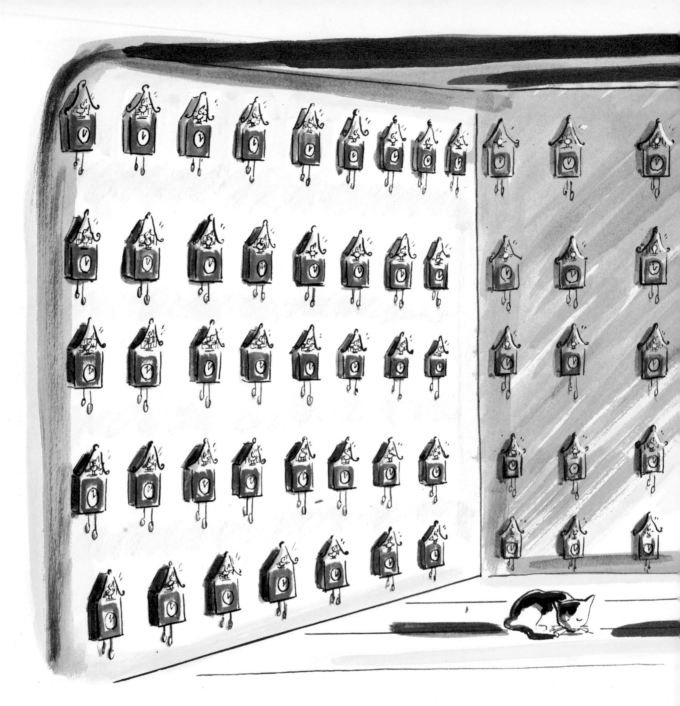

And the little cuckoos who lived in the clocks would hop out
and shout "Cuckoo" as hard as they could.

They would shout "Cuckoo" at one o'clock, and they shouted
"Cuckoo, Cuckoo" at two o'clock . . . and so on every hour

of the day and night.

All except one cuckoo. He was always a little late. His clock would strike with the others on the hour, but the cuckoo would not pop out with all the others and shout "Cuckoo."

He came out almost a minute after all the cuckoos had gone back into their clocks, and he would shout as loudly as he could, "Cuckoo," if it was past one o'clock or "Cuckoo, Cuckoo," if it was past two o'clock, and so on at each and every hour.

The village children on their way home from school would always stop at the clockmaker's shop to see and hear the cuckoos as they hopped out of their clocks.

And they waited anxiously for the late cuckoo to pop out of his clock, too. It always seemed like a long, long time before the late cuckoo came out. But at last out he would pop, shout his three "Cuckoo's" (for three o'clock), flap his wings, and hop back into his clock.

The village children would smile and nod at the old clock-maker in his window and then go home.

The old clockmaker would smile and shake his head at the late cuckoo as he said:

"Someday I must fix that little clock . . . yes, someday I will fix it."

But he never seemed to find the time to fix that clock. All the villagers knew about the late cuckoo. And if one of them came in to have his watch fixed or to buy a new cuckoo clock about the time the cuckoos were to pop out, he'd wait to see and hear them; then he'd wait one more minute for the late cuckoo to appear.

And then he'd smile and go chuckling home to tell his family that the late cuckoo had been late again.

But sometimes if a stranger came into the shop to buy a cuckoo clock and heard the late cuckoo, he'd shake his head.

"Your cuckoo clocks are not perfect," the stranger would say to the old clockmaker. "I think I'll look for a cuckoo clock in the next village."

Again the old clockmaker would say to himself:

"I must find time to fix that clock . . . I must find time . . ."

But he never did fix the clock until one very important day.

That was the day the Sultan of Garabia came riding into the little village high up in the Swiss Alps.

The very rich Sultan of Garabia, with an army of servants mounted on elephants, was traveling through Switzerland.

He would stop now and then to buy some presents to take home to his many nieces and nephews and dozens of cousins in Garabia. He had bought hundreds of boxes of fine Swiss chocolates, hundreds of yards of fine Swiss lace, and hundreds of warm woolen sweaters and mittens for his many nieces and nephews and dozens of cousins.

(Since it was very hot in Garabia, the Sultan's Chief Servant could not understand why the Sultan had bought all those warm sweaters and mittens. But he did not say what he thought because he knew that was not the best thing to do when dealing with Sultans.)

Now it so happened that the Sultan of Garabia, looking for something very special to buy, was riding through the village at the time the village children, just out of school, were gathered around the front window of the clock shop waiting for the cuckoo clocks to strike three.

"There must be something in that little shop that interests children," said the Sultan to his Chief Servant. "Let us stop and look."

The Sultan and his Chief Servant dismounted from their elephants and joined the children in front of the little clock shop.

"Cuckoo clocks!" cried the Sultan. "What lovely cuckoo clocks! I am sure my nieces and nephews and dozens of cousins will be delighted with them if I bring these clocks back to Garabia. I shall go in and buy them at once."

And with that, the Sultan, followed by his Chief Servant, marched right into the little clockmaker's shop.

"Clockmaker," said the Sultan, "how many cuckoo clocks do you have here?"

The old clockmaker said:

"I am not sure, Your Highness . . . I have not counted them lately . . . . But if you give me time I'll count them right now."

The Sultan nodded his head.

"You may count them," he said.

The old clockmaker got a pencil and a pad of paper and then he counted all his clocks. He wrote down the number on his pad.

"There you are, Your Highness. There are exactly one hundred and twenty-three clocks hanging in my shop."

"I think I will need them all," said the Sultan. "Please let me have your pencil and paper. I'd like to add up how many nieces and nephews and dozens of cousins I have."

The old clockmaker gave the Sultan his paper and pencil. After a moment of scribbling the Sultan cried aloud.

"That's exactly right! I have one hundred and twenty-two nieces and nephews and cousins . . . that leaves one clock for me . . . I shall buy them all right now."

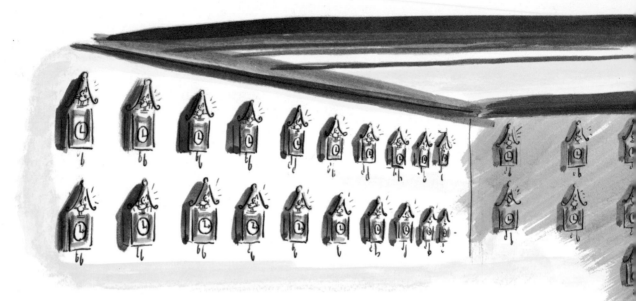

Just then the minute hands of all the clocks moved and it was exactly three o'clock. And the little cuckoos hopped out of their clocks and shouted:

"Cuckoo . . . Cuckoo . . . Cuckoo . . . !"

It was a wonderful sound to hear and a beautiful sight to see!

"These clocks are wonderful . . . all exactly right. Yes, I shall buy them at once," cried the Sultan. "Wrap them up, please. I'll take them with me."

The Sultan snapped his fingers and his Chief Servant reached into his pocket and brought out the Sultan's huge purse, which he was allowed to carry.

"Shall I pay you with gold or would you rather have diamonds and rubies for your wonderful clocks?" asked the Sultan.

"Oh, dear me!" said the old clockmaker (he was bewildered by his good fortune); "I suppose gold would be nice . . . but I do like rubies . . ."

And at that moment . . . just a minute after three . . . the late cuckoo popped out of his clock, flapped his wings, and shouted, "Cuckoo . . . Cuckoo . . . Cuckoo . . ."

"What's this?" exclaimed the Sultan. "Your clocks are not all exactly right . . . . Perhaps only that one is right and the others are all wrong! Or is that one wrong and are all the others right?"

"Oh, Your Highness," said the old clockmaker, "I must explain."

The Sultan raised his hand and silenced him.

"I am not sure now that any of your clocks is right . . . I will not buy any of them."

"Your Highness, please listen to me," cried the old clock-maker. "Only that one little cuckoo is wrong . . . . He is always a little late . . . . I've been meaning to fix him, but I did not have the time . . . . Your Highness, if you will honor my shop with another visit tomorrow morning, I am sure I can fix that cuckoo clock by then . . . and you will see all my clocks will be exactly right."

The Sultan thought a moment.

"Very well, I shall return just before ten o'clock tomorrow morning," said the Sultan.

Then he and his Chief Servant left the little clock shop, walked through the crowd of children in front of the shop window, and mounted their elephants. And they rode off to the castle the Sultan had rented for the few days he planned to stay in the little Swiss village.

Now the village children looking in the shop window did not nod and smile at the old clockmaker as they usually did. The clockmaker was very sad as he looked at the late cuckoo's clock and they were sad with him. They quietly crowded into his shop.

"I must really fix that little clock now," said the old clock-maker. "I wonder what can be wrong with it."

"Perhaps the spring is loose," said one boy quietly.

"Or perhaps the wheels are worn out," said another.

"Maybe there's a little dust in it," said a third.

And other children, both boys and girls, thought of other things that might be wrong with the clock.

But the old clockmaker just shook his head sadly and kept staring at the late cuckoo clock.

"Maybe . . . just maybe," said a little girl after a long silence, "maybe the little cuckoo really falls asleep in the clock . . . . Maybe he should be awakened just before it is time to pop out."

For a moment or two no one said anything. Then, one by one, or two by two, the children left the clockmaker's shop and sadly walked home.

Now the little clockmaker was all alone.

"Well, there's only one thing to do," he said to himself. "I must fix that clock."

He took the late cuckoo's clock off the wall and put it on his workbench.

"What shall I do first?" he asked himself. "Perhaps the spring is loose, as the children said."

He took the spring out of the clock and cleaned it thoroughly. Then he wound it up tight and put it back into the clock again.

Then he moved the hand of the clock around to the number four. But the little cuckoo did not pop out in time. He was late again . . . even later than he had been before.

"Well, that's not it," said the old clockmaker. "Perhaps the wheels are worn out . . ."

He took all the wheels out of the clock and looked at each one carefully. Then he filed and polished them and put them all back where they belonged. That took a long time. Now again he moved the hands of the clock around to five o'clock . . . and again the little cuckoo did not come out on time.

This time he was later than ever!

"Surely *that's* not the trouble with the clock," said the old clockmaker.

He tried everything and did everything that he remembered the children had said . . . late into the night.

But the things he did did not improve the clock. In fact, the little cuckoo came out later and later.

And at last the little cuckoo did not come out at all!

"Now I've done it," said the old clockmaker sadly. "I've ruined the clock completely . . . At least the cuckoo did come out, even though he was a little late, before I fixed it . . . . Now he won't come out at all! I wonder why."

The old clockmaker carefully opened the little door out of which the little cuckoo used to hop . . . a little late.

He peeked into the darkness in the clock and he saw the little cuckoo . . . . *The little cuckoo was fast asleep!*

"Oh, that's it . . . He really *does* go to sleep in the clock, as the little girl said," the old clockmaker whispered to himself as he carefully closed the door.

"Now, how shall I wake him up just before it's time to pop out?" asked the old clockmaker.

He thought and thought and thought.

"I have it," he cried at last.

Then he quickly went to work. He worked very late. At last, near midnight, he was finished. He went to bed and slept peacefully through the night, knowing that the little cuckoo would never be late again.

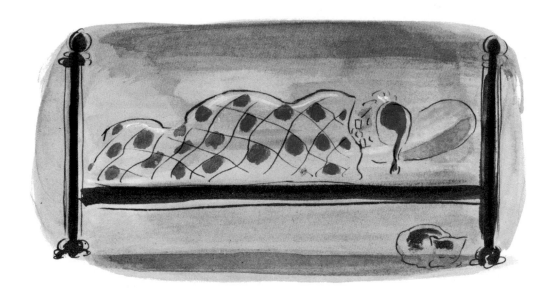

The next morning was a holiday. There was no school. The village children came to peek into the clockmaker's window. The old clockmaker was cheerfully bustling about his shop. He waved to the children and they waved to him.

A few minutes before ten o'clock the Sultan and his Chief Servant rode their elephants down from his rented castle to the clockmaker's shop.

"Good morning, clockmaker," said the Sultan as he came into the shop. "Have you fixed your clocks? . . . Are they all right now?"

"Good morning, Your Highness," said the old clockmaker cheerfully. "Yes, Your Highness, they are all right, exactly right . . . every one of them."

"Very well," said the Sultan, "we shall see . . . we shall see."

Then he snapped his fingers.

"I would sit down as I wait," he said to his Chief Servant.

The Chief Servant dashed out of the clockmaker's shop and was back in a moment with an armful of silk cushions. He piled them up on the floor of the shop and the Sultan sat on the silk cushions waiting until the clocks struck ten.

The village children peeking into the clockmaker's shop waited anxiously, too.

Three minutes before ten . . . two before ten . . . one before ten . . . and then . . .

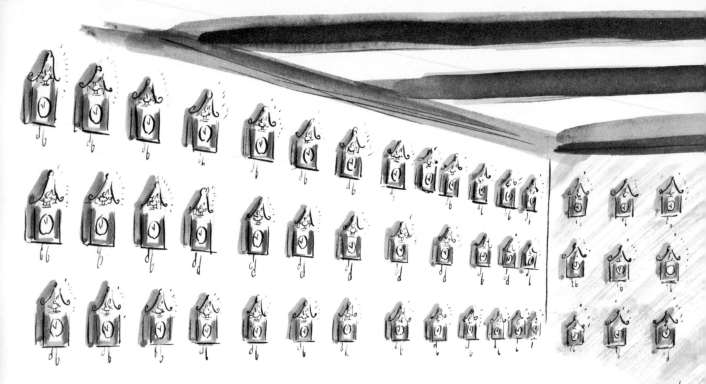

. . . TEN O'CLOCK!

Out popped all the cuckoos at exactly the same instant . . . every one of them, even the late cuckoo! And they shouted:

"Cuckoo . . . Cuckoo . . . Cuckoo . . . Cuckoo . . . Cuckoo . . .

"Cuckoo . . . Cuckoo . . . Cuckoo . . . Cuckoo . . . Cuckoo . . ." all together!

"Wonderful!" shouted the Sultan. "Your clocks are exactly right. . . . They are perfect! . . . I'll buy them all!"

He snapped his fingers and his Chief Servant rushed forward holding the Sultan's purse already open.

The children outside the shop window shouted, "Hurrah!"

"Will you have gold or diamonds and rubies for your clocks, clockmaker?" cried the Sultan.

"I guess I'd better take gold . . . even though I do like rubies," said the old clockmaker. "And, Your Highness, there's just one more thing I must tell you. . . ."

"What is that, my good man?" asked the Sultan.

"Well . . . well . . . Your Highness," said the old clockmaker slowly, "I can only sell you one hundred and twenty-two of these clocks. . . . One I must keep for myself. . . ."

The Sultan frowned.

"But, Your Highness, I will make you another cuckoo clock . . . a beautiful clock. I will make one in just a few days with your own rubies and diamonds all over it . . . if you want it that way. Then you will have one hundred and twenty-three clocks. . . . The most beautiful one will be for you.''

The Sultan thought a moment. Then he said:

"Very well, clockmaker. Here is the gold for the one hundred and twenty-two clocks. Wrap them up. I'll take them with me now . . . and, clockmaker, here are some rubies, diamonds, and other jewels for my own clock.''

The old clockmaker wrapped up all the cuckoo clocks except the one in which the late cuckoo lived. Then the Chief Servant carried them out and piled them on his elephant. And, at last, he and the Sultan of Garabia rode away to the Sultan's rented castle.

The moment they were gone the village children danced into the clockmaker's shop. The children were as happy about the old clockmaker's good fortune as he was.

"Now," said the clockmaker, "since you children were so helpful yesterday, I must show you the secret . . . . I must show you how and why the late cuckoo popped out in time. Now remember, this is a secret. . . ."

When all the children had gathered around, the old clockmaker carefully opened the little door of the clock.

The children peeped in. There, in the clock's darkness, they could see the little cuckoo fast asleep. And they all could see that right near the little cuckoo's sleepy head there was another clock—a tiny little clock!

It was the tiniest, littlest clock anyone had ever seen.

"Do you all see that little clock in there?" whispered the old clockmaker softly so he would not wake up the little cuckoo. "Well, that's a little alarm clock. It is set to go off just a minute before the hour. That's what wakes the cuckoo up. And now I am sure the little late cuckoo will never be late again."

The children were delighted.

"Of course," the old clockmaker went on, "I could not sell this one to the Sultan. I don't believe he or anyone else but I could wind it up properly . . . . I will never sell this clock to anyone."

And the clockmaker did make a fine new clock for the Sultan. It was all covered with rubies and diamonds and other jewels.

But that special cuckoo clock—the one with the little alarm clock inside it to awaken the cuckoo—was never sold to anyone. And no one but the children and the old clockmaker (and the people who read this book) will ever know the secret . . . how the late cuckoo popped out of his clock in time to shout:

"Cuckoo . . . Cuckoo . . . Cuckoo . . . Cuckoo . . . Cuckoo . . .

"Cuckoo . . . Cuckoo . . . Cuckoo . . . Cuckoo . . . Cuckoo . . . at exactly the right minute at ten o'clock every morning from then on . . . forever after!